Order this book online at www.trafford.com
or email orders@trafford.com

Most Trafford titles are also available at major online book retailers.

Printed in the United States of America.

ISBN: 978-1-4907-4687-6 (sc)
        978-1-4907-4686-9 (e)

Library of Congress Control Number: 2014916997

Our mission is to efficiently provide the world's finest, most comprehensive book publishing service, enabling every author to experience
success. To find out how to publish your book, your way, and have it available worldwide, visit us online at www.trafford.com

Any people depicted in stock imagery provided by Thinkstock are models,
and such images are being used for illustrative purposes only.
Certain stock imagery © Thinkstock.

Trafford rev. 09/23/2014

www.trafford.com
North America & international
toll-free: 1 888 232 4444 (USA & Canada)
fax: 812 355 4082

HAVE YOU EVER?

Laura Spearman ☺

By **Laura Spearman**

Illustrations by **Windel Eborlas**

Have you ever seen a camel with
a roller-coaster hump?

Did you buckle up and ride his back
while shouting, "THUMPY-LUMP!"?

Did his frizzy fur fly backwards as you
screeched down each steep hill?

Did you throw your head back
laughing merrily at every thrill?

Well, I met that kooky camel
as I lay asleep last night,

And I had a ton of fun up
until the morning light.

Have you ever seen a gerbil on
a surfboard on the sea?

Was she riding giant waves while
she clapped her paws with glee?

Did she then roll on the sand and
roar with laughter in the sun?

Did she dry off with a seaweed towel,
so proud of what she'd done?

Well, I met that giant gerbil in
my sleep two nights ago,

And I hope I see her at that beach
the next time that I go.

Have you ever seen a pony
eating pizza slice by slice?

Was he able to chow down while
skating on a lake's thin ice?

Did he bravely glide and slide and
whirl and twirl beneath the moon?

Did he take a bow, then gallop home,
but plan to go back soon?

Well, I watched that pony's horseplay
in my sleeping three nights past,

And I loved his show and wished that
it would last and last and last.

Have you ever seen an elephant
who loved to wear tutus?

Were her four pink ballet slippers 'specially
made? (WOW, AWESOME SHOES!)

Did she dance with grace and with
no fear that anyone would boo?

Did a crowd of calves stand, clap, and
cheer as soon as she was through?

Well, in my dreams four nights
ago, I had a front-row seat . . .

And I'd love to meet that pachyderm
again 'cause she was *sweet!*

Have you ever seen an ostrich with
a neck that reached the stars?

Could he stretch his neck like crazy?
Did he stretch it way past Mars?

Could he twist it up the way clowns
twist up long, skinny balloons?

Did his neck become a dog, a
cat, a mouse, or a baboon?

Well, in my sleep five nights ago,
I met that long-necked bird.

I shook his wing and yelled, "Well done!" . . .
He screamed, "Thanks!" when he heard.

Have you ever met a cuddly bear
who wouldn't harm a fly?

A bear so very gentle that sad
movies made him cry?

When you told him you were "cold,"
did he hug you back to "warm?"

Did he promise that he'd keep you safe
through each and every storm?

Well, that bear became my lifelong
friend when we met six nights past.

I'll see him every time I sleep;
I know our bond will last.

Have you ever met my mommy,
seen her tuck me in each night?

All seven nights a week, I mean;
my mommy holds me tight.

She reads and sings and says, "Sweet Dreams";
she helps me say a prayer . . .

I watch her green eyes twinkle as
her cheek-kiss warms the air.

Because of her, I'm safe and warm
and dry . . . That's how I feel.

I'm free to dream of make-believe,
'cause Mommy's love is REAL.

CPSIA information can be obtained at www.ICGtesting.com
Printed in the USA
BVOW10s2029061014

369751BV00005B/7/P